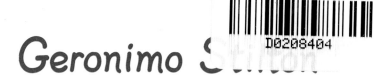

Geronimo Stilton

THE LITTLE BOOK OF HAPPINESS

Scholastic Inc.

ISBN 978-0-545-48255-4

Based on an original idea by Elisabetta Dami.

www.geronimostilton.com

Published by Scholastic Inc., 557 Broadway, New York, NY 10012.
SCHOLASTIC and associated logos are trademarks and/or registered trademarks of Scholastic Inc.

Stilton is the name of a famous English cheese. It is a registered trademark of the Stilton Cheese Makers' Association. For more information, go to www.stiltoncheese.com.

Text by Geronimo Stilton
Original title *Il piccolo libro della felicità*
Cover by Larry Keys
Illustrations by Wally Bluecheese
Graphics by Merenguita Gingermouse and Superpao

Special thanks to AnnMarie Anderson
Translated by Julia Heim
Interior design by Becky James

12 11 10 9 8 7   15 16 17 18/0

Printed in the U.S.A.   40
First printing, January 2013

THE SCENT OF FLOWERS

It had been a very busy day at the office, and I was feeling **grumpy**. I was **exhausted**, and I couldn't wait to get home and take a **relaxing** cheddar-scented bubble bath.

Oh, excuse me! I didn't introduce myself. My name is Stilton, *Geronimo Stilton*. I am the editor of *The Rodent's Gazette*, the most famouse newspaper on Mouse Island.

As I was saying, I walked in the door — and found my house full of mice.

MOLDY MOZZARELLA! I had completely forgotten that it was my dear nephew Benjamin's birthday.

I was throwing a party to celebrate!

A few hours later, my grumpy mood was gone, and my heart was **bursting** with joy. We had just polished off the last crumb of gorgonzola **birthday cake**, and my guests were relaxing around a **LONG** table. Then my sister, Thea, suggested that we all go out to the garden to admire the *starry night sky*.

The taste of gorgonzola and the scent of flowers in the air brought back memories of many other happy nights spent together with the mice I love.

Happy birthday, Benjamin!

I sighed. Ah, how wonderful it was to be surrounded by my friends and family! My **ROUGH** day at the office was completely forgotten.

Benjamin **squeezed** my paw.

"There are so many **stars**, Uncle Geronimo," he said. "The sky seems like it's made of velvet. And the moon is *shining* so brightly! What a perfect birthday."

I gave him a kiss on the tip of his snout.

"Keep this memory in your **heart**," I told

Oh, how brightly the stars are shining tonight!

him. "Happy moments are precious jewels that become more valuable as time passes."

Benjamin and I shared a smile. "It's important to recognize happiness, as it's too easy to get caught up in everyday life," I told him as I thought back to my day at work. "Sometimes we don't take the time to enjoy the little things, like the scent of flowers on a starry night. Or the big things, like the affection of those who love you!"

I gave Benjamin a hug. The air was chilly, so I covered him with my jacket.

He became quiet and thoughtful.

"Uncle Geronimo, what is happiness?" he asked.

"Well, it's difficult to describe," I told him, "but I'll do my BEST!" And I will do my best to explain it to you, too, my dear mouse friends reading this book!

LIFE IS A TRUE TREASURE!

Every mouse looks for happiness in life.
But often, **mice** don't realize how many
different reasons there are to be happy. They
just need to **LOOK** around and see all of the
beautiful **gifts** that life gives them . . . .

**The beginning of
a new day!**

**A mother's
affection!**

**A father's
encouragement!**

True friendship!

The beauty of nature!

Meeting new friends!

A great love that lasts forever!

Looking at a starry sky together!

Do you see how many **wonderful** things there are in life? Just keep your heart open to new adventures, and await the future with **joy** and **hope**. Each day is a gift — life is a *true* treasure!

WHAT HELPS US GROW?

Benjamin and I continued to walk around the garden. We stopped to admire a **great oak tree**.

"Look at this tree!" Benjamin exclaimed. "Its roots are so **DEEP**, its branches are so **strong**, and its leaves are so **THICK!**" and I picked up an acorn.

"It took years for this oak tree to grow," I said thoughtfully. "Once, it was just a **tiny** acorn."

"What made this oak so **big**?" Benjamin asked. "The nutrients from the **EARTH** it lives in and the slow alternation between **sun** and RAIN and **wind** and snow all help the tree grow tall," I said. "The same thing happens with us! When we are born, we are tiny mice. It takes years for us to become **big**! What is it that really helps us **GROW**? It's everything: the good things and the bad, the happy times and the sad ones. Every experience — even **pain** — makes us stronger, because it is a part of life."

The oak tree and I grew up together!

THE THOUSAND COLORS OF HAPPINESS

Benjamin looked up at me, his eyes BRIGHT.

"Why is it that sometimes I feel happy, and sometimes I feel sad?" he asked.

"It's normal to feel many **DIFFERENT** emotions at different times," I told him. "It's natural — it's like the fact that sunlight, which seems white, is actually made of many **different** colors. Do you know how a rainbow is made?"

Benjamin shook his head.

"After a storm, **thousands** of water droplets remain suspended in the sky," I explained. "The **sunlight** passes through the drops and separates into seven colors: **red**, **orange**, **yellow**, **green**, **blue**, **indigo**, and **violet**. This creates a shining **rainbow** in the gray sky!"

Experiment

Ask an adult to help you with this experiment. Make a ray of sunlight pass through a prism. You will notice that the light seems white, but in reality it is made up of seven different colors!

Ray of sunlight

Prism

"It's okay if your emotions change, too," I continued. "Learn to recognize your feelings and calmly accept them, because they are a part of you. FEAR, sadness, happiness, joy, and LOVE are all important feelings. No matter what you are feeling, accept it — if you accept every part of yourself, you will be truly **happy**!"

"But what if I can't always do that, Uncle?" Benjamin asked.

"Well, no mouse is perfect!" I said with a smile. "Don't be ashamed to make mistakes. Growing means recognizing your mistakes and trying to change and better yourself.

"Have the courage to apologize for your mistakes and to FORGIVE those who make mistakes that affect you! You will find that the more a heart is able to FORGIVE, the more it is able to *love*."

Anger, resentment, and envy are negative feelings that weigh us down. Try to fill your heart with joy, and it will become happy and light, as though it has wings!

If you feel sad, look for someone who can help! Turn to your mom, your dad, your teacher, or a friend ... someone big or small who knows how to listen to you. Don't keep quiet! Every problem has a solution, and it's easier to find one if you talk about it with those around you.

HAPPINESS IS CONTAGIOUS!

I remembered my **ROUGH** day at the office.

"It's important to remember that emotions can spread easily," I told Benjamin. "Happiness is **contagious**: When we are **happy**, we share our good mood. But **unhappiness** is also contagious: When we have a long face, we can make others feel **sad**, too.

"The best gift we can give is a big smile!"

NEGATIVE ENERGY

Grrrr!   Humph!

POSITIVE ENERGY

How are you?   I'm great, thanks!

> Happiness generates more happiness, just as a stone thrown in a pond creates a wave that spreads on and on.

Groucho Marx

(American comedian and film star, 1890–1977)

"I, not events, have the power to make me happy or unhappy today. I can choose which it shall be. Yesterday is dead, tomorrow hasn't arrived yet. I have just one day, today, and I'm going to be happy in it."

Charles M. Schulz

(American cartoonist of Peanuts, 1922–200

"Happiness is a warm puppy."

George Sand

(French novelist, 1804–1876)

"There is only one happiness in life: to love and be loved!"

Aristotle

(Greek philosopher, 384–322 BC

"Happiness depends upon ourselves."

Eleanor Roosevelt

(American author, politician, activist, and First Lady, 1884–1962)

"Happiness is not a goal; it is a by-product."

Robert Louis Stevenson

(Scottish novelist, 1850–1894)

"There is no duty we so much underrate as the duty to be happy!"

Albert Einstein

(German physicist, 1879–1955)
"The man who regards his own life and that of his fellow creatures as meaningless is not merely unfortunate, but almost disqualified for life."

Mark Twain

(American author and humorist, 1835–1910)
"To get the full value of joy you must have someone to divide it with."

Audrey Hepburn

(British actress and humanitarian, 1929–1993)
"I heard a definition once: Happiness is health and a short memory! I wish I'd invented it, because it is very true."

Horace

(Roman poet, 65–8 BC)
"Carpe diem!"
(Seize the day!)

Henry David Thoreau

(American author, poet, and philosopher, 1817–1862)
"There is no value in life except what you choose to place upon it and no happiness in any place except what you bring to it yourself."

Benjamin Franklin

(American author, politician, scientist, and inventor, 1706–1790)
"Money has never made man happy, nor will it; there is nothing in its nature to produce happiness. The more of it one has the more one wants."

WE ARE ALL TIME TRAVELERS. . . .

"Life is a really **LONG** journey that lasts for years and years, like a finely aged **cheese**," I told Benjamin. "But at the same time it is very **short**, because the span of each life is nothing compared to **eternity**."

We can travel all over the world searching for happiness, but only in our hearts can we look for and find it!

"We are all time travelers," I said thoughtfully. "We are all in search of something to give sense to our existence."

I pointed at the SKY above us.

"Every mouse wants to know: *What is the meaning of life?*" I told Benjamin. "There are as many different answers as there are stars in the SKY. Everyone gives a different answer based on family, on his or her nationality, RELIGION, life experience, and personality. But since we are all together on this voyage, it's important to get along, despite our different beliefs!"

Benjamin nodded his head.

"Picture a big pot of fondue," I explained. "Every mouse's answer to this question is like a different cheese. Blended TOGETHER, the different cheeses create a dish that's tastier than each cheese on its own!"

THE LIGHT OF HOPE

"I know it's important to be **happy**, Uncle," Benjamin said sweetly. "But what do I do when something **sad** happens?"

"That's a very **good** question," I replied. "It's true that in every life, there will be **difficult** moments. A person whom you *love* may have to leave you, or someone might get very sick. How do we talk about happiness then? The important thing is not to forget the happy moments lived and those that are still to come. Don't give yourself over to the **HARD** times — continue to **believe** in the future. Keep **faith** that life can change for the better. The light of hope is always lit, for you and for others!"

Just one light is enough to keep hope for many.

Live by example.
Try to make the
world better for
yourself and
for others!

LIFE IS SO SWEET!

To further explain my point, I told Benjamin this ancient legend:

"A FARMER RAN THROUGH A DARK FOREST, CHASED BY A FEROCIOUS TIGER. SUDDENLY, HE FOUND HIMSELF AT THE EDGE OF A HUGE CLIFF! HE SLIPPED OVER THE EDGE AND GRABBED HOLD OF A STRONG ROOT. AS HE HELD ON, SUSPENDED IN MIDAIR, HE REALIZED THAT A TINY MOUSE WAS NIBBLING AT THE ROOT. THEN THE FARMER SAW A RIPE, RED STRAWBERRY. WITH ONE HAND CLUTCHING THE ROOT, HE REACHED FOR THE STRAWBERRY. HE TASTED IT AND SMILED. *LIFE IS SO SWEET!* HE THOUGHT. . . ."

"I don't **understand**, Uncle," Benjamin said. "What happened to the **FARMER**?"

"The legend ends there!" I told him. "The point of the story is to illustrate how **IMPORTANT** it is to always hold on to happiness, especially during hard times."

HAPPINESS

For the love of cheese, how quickly this moment passes!

You see, dear readers, happiness is in everything: in food when we are **hungry**, in a smile when we feel **alone** ... **everything** can be happiness. It's up to us to grab on to every **moment of joy** that life offers!

Are you happy at this moment? If you are, do something nice! Hug someone near you or call a friend to tell him "life is wonderful!"

LOVE MAKES THE
WORLD GO ROUND!

Let's fuel the Earth with the purest energy there is: love!

We often hear **bad** news on television or in the newspaper. But every day there is a lot of **good news** in the world, too. We need to share the good news: It is up to **US** to change things!

You can decide what news really counts. When you see something **BEAUTIFUL** and **good** happening around you, tell others! You can spread *optimism*. It's good for you, and it's good for others as well!

And when bad news **SCARES** you, be sure you talk about that with an adult, too. Go to your **mom**, your **DAD**, a **teacher**, or another trusted adult and tell that person how you're **FEELING**. You don't need to feel **alone**: You can overcome your **fears**!

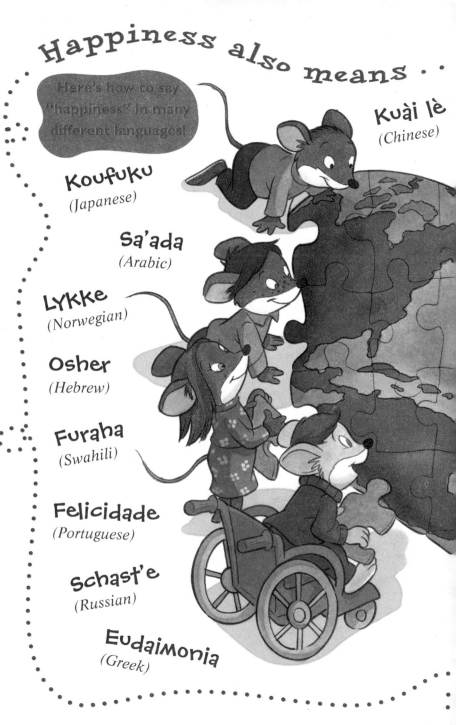

Happiness also means...

Here's how to say "happiness" in many different languages!

Kuài lè
(Chinese)

Koufuku
(Japanese)

Sa'ada
(Arabic)

Lykke
(Norwegian)

Osher
(Hebrew)

Furaha
(Swahili)

Felicidade
(Portuguese)

Schast'e
(Russian)

Eudaimonia
(Greek)

THE SECRET FORMULA FOR KINDNESS

Put a **SECRET FORMULA** for kindness into practice! Do something nice for those around you every day. Set the table or take the dog for a **walk** without being asked, or help your little brother with his **homework**. Offering your **help** is the easiest way to make those around you **happy**. Helping others will also make you feel **useful** and happy yourself!

SECRET FORMULA:
Treat others as you
would like to be
treated!

So Many Beautiful Colors . . .

The world is like a carpet made of many *different-colored strands of thread.* Each strand symbolizes someone in the world, and each strand is different from the others because of **culture**, **customs**, and *traditions*. These differences make the carpet **PRECIOUS** and **unique**!

There are so many beautiful colors!

FRIENDSHIP IS AN ANCHOR

"Benjamin, do you know the expression, 'HE WHO FINDS A FRIEND FINDS A TREASURE'?" I asked my nephew.

He shook his head.

"Well, now you do!" I said.

He smiled. Friends are truly **valuable**: In difficult times they can help you **OVERCOME** problems. And in happy times they share your **JOY**!

Friendship is a secure **ANCHOR** during the **storms** of life.

Together with a friend, we can do things that seem impossible to do alone.

A SMILE IS A MAGICAL KEY

A smile doesn't cost a thing, but it is a magical **KEY** capable of opening doors. Try to **SMILE** more often at the people around you. You will notice that every smile is **SPECIAL**: It conveys your emotions and helps you communicate better with others. Every smile is a message of happiness. So go ahead and **smile**! Chances are others will smile back at you, even when things are **tough**. You'll be spreading **happiness** by moving just a few small muscles.

Humph!

Come on, smile!

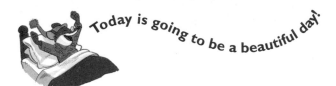
Today is going to be a beautiful day!

HAPPINESS GLASSES

Pessimism is like a pair of glasses with **gray** lenses, through which you can only see the world in **BLACK** and **WHITE**. Optimism, on the other hand, is like a pair of glasses with **rainbow** lenses: When you put them on, life is in **color**! Every morning when you wake up, it's up to you to **CHOOSE** which pair of glasses to put on for the day. *You decide how you will see the world!*

To put on happiness glasses each day, think about all of the things in life that you do have, not the things you don't.

Don't look at life in black and white ...

... look at life in color!

THE RECIPE FOR HAPPINESS

Is there a recipe for happiness? Only **you** can discover your recipe, because only **you** can know what will make you *truly* happy.

Do you want to know my personal recipe? Here it is!

You must know what makes you truly happy!

THE RECIPE FOR HAPPINESS

- Learn to love yourself, because only then is it possible to love other people.
  - Understand which things really matter in life.
  - Look on the bright side of every situation.
  - Add a good dose of patience, a bunch of humor, and a ton of optimism!
- Finally, top things off with a pinch of trustworthy friends!

？

THE GLASS TEST

Look closely at this glass. Do you think it is HALF FULL or **half empty**? What kind of mouse are you?

OPTIMIST

If you said the glass is HALF FULL, you tend to focus on the positives in your life. You are probably happy, enthusiastic, and you have a lot of interests — and a lot of friends. Congratulations!

PESSIMIST

If you said the glass is **half empty**, you tend to focus on the negatives in life. Why not try to change things around? Make friends with someone who seems lonely, or do something kind for a friend. If you help someone else look on the bright side of things, chances are you'll feel happier, too!

THOUSANDS OF REASONS TO BE HAPPY!

How many reasons are there to be happy? There are **thousands**! Here are a few examples . . .

- The smell of **FRESHLY** baked bread!
- A **picnic** in springtime beside a stream!
- Walking **barefoot** in a field!
- Decorating a Christmas tree with **family**!
- A **song** that reminds you of a happy time!
- A **warm** blanket on a **cold** night!

A really big ice-cream sundae!

The first snowfall of winter!

A flower for someone special!

A warm bath with lots of bubbles!

Watching a sunset with someone!

Going to a concert for the first time!

- Making a **gift** with your own hands!
- Having breakfast in your *pajamas* on the weekend!
- The smell of an ocean breeze!
- Finishing your homework *faster* than you expected!
- Dozing on a blanket outdoors!
- The first rays of sun after a storm!
- Counting **shooting** stars on a summer night!
- Singing your favorite song in the shower!
- Going to the **movies** with your best friend!
- Walking on dry leaves in the **woods**!

- Dancing to **rock-and-roll** music!
- Making **FRIENDS** with a new classmate!
- Putting **photographs** in an album!
- Catching the bus right on **time**!
- A grandmother's **hug**!
- Placing the very last piece in a **puzzle**!
- Your **first** plane trip to a country far, far away!
- Drinking hot chocolate in front of a **cozy** fireplace!
- Learning to **dive** off a diving board!
- Waking up on a **sunny** day!

Sending a message in a bottle!

Hugging a tree really tight!

Being part of a team!

Sitting on the beach reading a book!

Finding a four-leaf clover!

A message that says I love you!

I ♥ U!

The first ski of the year!

A birthday cake!

-Waking up at dawn to realize that you still have three more hours to **sleep**!

- **Licking** an ice-cream cone as it drips!

- Dedicating a **poem** to a special person!

- Learning to ride a **bike**!

- Telling a **joke** that no one else knows!

- The **smell** of freshly cut grass!

- The last day of **SCHOOL**!

- Learning to play chess with your **grandfather**!

- **Daydreaming** about what you'll be when you grow up!

- Getting over a case of the **HICCUPS**!

- Telling a **secret** to a friend who understands you!
- **FINISHING** a crossword puzzle by yourself!
- Finding a *fantastic* website!
- An unexpected compliment that makes you **blush**!
- Leaving for a long **vacation**!
- **Returning** home after an adventurous trip!
- Someone who offers you help, not just **advice**!
- A **surprise** birthday party!
- A letter from a friend who **moved away**!
- **CHEERING** for your favorite team!

Smelling a rose!

Trying a new pizza!

Going to see a dinosaur exhibit!

Having a snowball fight!

Now It's Your Turn!

Now it's **your** turn!

On a separate sheet of paper, write a list of **ten** things that make you **happy**!

I think...

I think happiness is...

For me, it's...

MOUSE'S HONOR

It was getting late, and it was well past Benjamin's bedtime.

"Well, Nephew, I think it's time for bed," I told him.

Benjamin nodded as he let out a **sleepy** yawn. "I hope every birthday is as happy as this one, Uncle," he said sweetly.

"If you remember to stay **positive** and look on the **bright** side every day, then each birthday will be a happy one, I promise," I replied. "Mouse's honor, or my name isn't *Geronimo Stilton*!"

#1 Lost Treasure of the Emerald Eye

#2 The Curse of the Cheese Pyramid

#3 Cat and Mouse in a Haunted House

#4 I'm Too Fond of My Fur!

#5 Four Mice Deep in the Jungle

#6 Paws Off, Cheddarface!

#7 Red Pizzas for a Blue Count

#8 Attack of the Bandit Cats

#9 A Fabumouse Vacation for Geronimo

#10 All Because of a Cup of Coffee

#11 It's Halloween, You 'Fraidy Mouse!

#12 Merry Christmas, Geronimo!

#13 The Phantom of the Subway

#14 The Temple of the Ruby of Fire

#15 The Mona Mousa Code

#16 A Cheese-Colored Camper

#17 Watch Your Whiskers, Stilton!

#18 Shipwreck on the Pirate Islands

#19 My Name Is
Stilton, Geronimo
Stilton

#20 Surf's Up,
Geronimo!

#21 The Wild,
Wild West

#22 The Secret
of Cacklefur
Castle

A Christmas Tale

#23 Valentine's
Day Disaster

#24 Field Trip to
Niagara Falls

#25 The Search
for Sunken
Treasure

#26 The Mummy
with No Name

#27 The
Christmas Toy
Factory

#28 Wedding
Crasher

#29 Down and
Out Down Under

#30 The Mouse
Island Marathon

#31 The
Mysterious
Cheese Thief

Christmas
Catastrophe

#32 Valley of the
Giant Skeletons

#33 Geronimo
and the Gold
Medal Mystery

#34 Geronimo
Stilton, Secret
Agent

#35 A Very Merry
Christmas

#36 Geronimo's
Valentine

#37 The Race Across America

#38 A Fabumouse School Adventure

#39 Singing Sensation

#40 The Karate Mouse

#41 Mighty Mount Kilimanjaro

#42 The Peculiar Pumpkin Thief

#43 I'm Not a Supermouse!

#44 The Giant Diamond Robbery

#45 Save the White Whale!

#46 The Haunted Castle

#47 Run for the Hills, Geronimo!

#48 The Mystery in Venice

#49 The Way of the Samurai

#50 This Hotel is Haunted!

#51 The Enormouse Pearl Heist

THE KINGDOM OF FANTASY

THE QUEST FOR PARADISE: THE RETURN TO THE KINGDOM OF FANTASY

THE AMAZING VOYAGE: THE THIRD ADVENTURE IN THE KINGDOM OF FANTASY

THE DRAGON PROPHECY: THE FOURTH ADVENTURE IN THE KINGDOM OF FANTASY